S.W.I.T.C.H.

#14 Alligator Action

Books in the
S.W.I.T.C.H. series

S.W.I.T.C.H.

#14 Alligator Action

Ali Sparkes

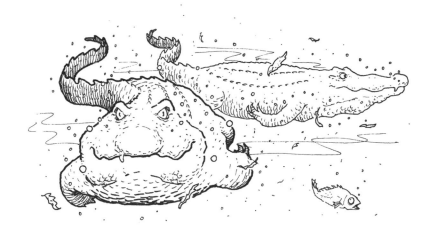

illustrated by
Ross Collins

MINNEAPOLIS

Darby Creek
A division of Lerner Publishing Group, Inc.
241 First Avenue North
Minneapolis, MN 55401 U.S.A.

For reading levels and more invormation, look up this title at www.lernerbooks.com.

Main body text set in ITC Goudy Sans Std. 14/19.
Typeface provided by Monotype Typography.

Library of Congress Cataloging-in-Publication Data
Sparkes, Ali.
    Alligator action / by Ali Sparkes ; illustrated by Ross Collins.
        pages   cm. — (S.W.I.T.C.H. ; #14)
    Summary: When Petty Potts disappears, twins Danny and Josh search her secret laboratory and house, where they find an irresistible bottle of S.W.I.T.C.H. spray, and later they find themselves on a live television talk show.
        ISBN 978–1–4677–2117–2 (lib. bdg. : alk. paper)
        ISBN 978–1–4677–2414–2 (eBook)
        [1. Missing persons—Fiction. 2. Television talk shows—Fiction. 3. Alligators—Fiction. 4. Brothers—Fiction. 5. Twins—Fiction. 6. Science fiction.] I. Collins, Ross, illustrator. II. Title.
PZ7.S73712All 2014
[Fic]—dc23   2013019718

Manufactured in the United States of America
1 – SB – 12/31/13

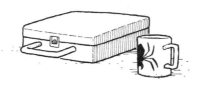

For Aled Lloyd Houston

With grateful thanks to
John Buckley and Dorothy Driver of
Amphibian and Reptile Conservation
for their hot-blooded guidance on
S.W.I.T.C.H.'s cold-blooded reptile heroes

Danny and Josh and Petty

Josh and Danny might be twins, but they're NOT the same.
Josh loves getting his hands dirty and learning about nature.
Danny thinks Josh is a nerd. Skateboarding and climbing are
way cooler! And their next-door neighbor, Petty, is only
interested in one thing . . . her top secret S.W.I.T.C.H. potion.

Danny
- FULL NAME: Danny Phillips
- AGE: eight years
- HEIGHT: taller than Josh
- FAVORITE THING: skateboarding
- WORST THING: creepy-crawlies and tidying
- AMBITION: to be a stuntman

Josh

- FULL NAME: Josh Phillips
- AGE: eight years
- HEIGHT: taller than Danny
- FAVORITE THING: collecting insects
- WORST THING: skateboarding
- AMBITION: to be an entomologist

Petty

- FULL NAME: Petty Hortense Potts
- AGE: none of your business
- HEIGHT: head and shoulders above every other scientist
- FAVORITE THING: S.W.I.T.C.H.ing Josh & Danny
- WORST THING: evil ex-friend Victor Crouch
- AMBITION: adoration and recognition as the world's most genius scientist (and for the government to say sorry!)

Contents

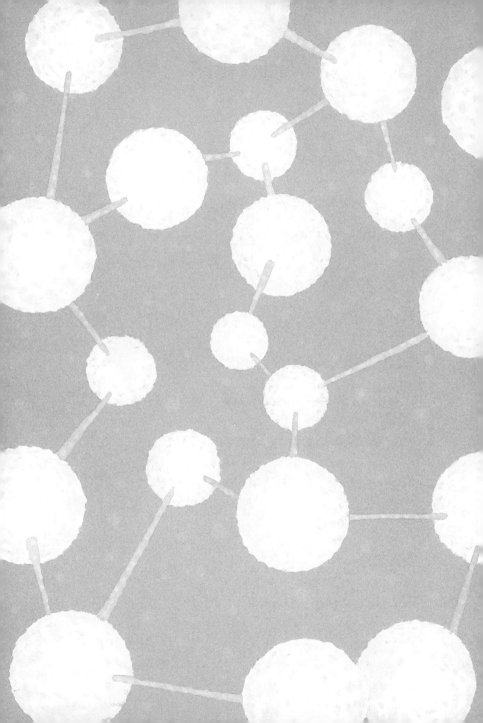

Missing Scientist . . .

"9-1-1. Which service do you require?"

"Police! Ambulance! Fire and Rescue . . . all of them!" Danny said.

"What is the nature of your emergency?"

"This old lady we know has vanished, and we think she's been kidnapped—or killed—or . . . or both!"

"What is your name and address, caller?"

"Eerrrm," Danny said. "Well . . . it's kind of secret!"

"Is this a prank call?"

"NO! It's just that . . . she's a genius scientist who can S.W.I.T.C.H. humans into spiders and frogs and snakes, and we're her assistants, and we have to keep it secret . . . and . . ."

"Young man, prank calls put other people's

lives at risk! If we hear from this number again, there will be trouble. I'm hanging up now."

CLICK. Burrrrrrrrrrrrrrrrrrrrrrrrrrrrrrrrrrrrrrr.

"That went well, then," Josh said, who had heard it all on speakerphone. "I told you it'd be no good! Nobody is going to believe us!"

Danny slumped down in the hallway and hung up the phone with a sigh. Josh was right. How could they ever explain what was really happening? Nobody would believe the truth—that their next-door neighbor was not just a slightly dotty old lady but, in fact, a genius scientist who had developed an amazing S.W.I.T.C.H. spray that could turn people into creepy-crawlies and amphibians and reptiles. He and Josh knew it was true—because they *were* the people Petty had S.W.I.T.C.H.ed. More times than they could count.

"Come on," Josh said, peering at the computer print-out in his hand. "Let's go down to the den. We need to think."

They walked out to the garden and found their way into the rhododendron bush. Piddle, their pet terrier, ran in behind them and sat between Josh and Danny, wagging his tail energetically, hoping for a ball game.

Danny took the computer printout from his brother and anxiously scratched his spiky blond hair as he read Petty Potts's last diary entry.

When it looked as if Petty still hadn't come back to her house after three days in a row, he and Josh had gotten so worried that they'd gone to check in the parking lot at Princessland—the girls' toys and frocks superstore over which Petty rented an attic—the location of her new secret laboratory. They had spotted Petty's old station wagon there. So they'd crept through Princessland to the lobby at the back and used the only S.W.I.T.C.H. spray they had—GeckoSWITCH. They had shrunk down to agile lizards and crawled through a gap under the locked door that led to Petty's lab.

In the lab, as soon as they'd S.W.I.T.C.H.ed back to boys again, they could see signs of a struggle . . . and Petty's diary entry still on her computer! She had been speaking her diary into a microphone—using a special program to convert her voice into words on-screen. It was the very last bit which had horrified Josh and Danny.

. . . my S.W.I.T.C.H. formula saved a life today! Josh, Danny, and Charlie ended up S.W.I.T.C.H.ing into green anacondas to rescue one of the girls from Charlie's school after she fell into the river.

But all of this pales into insignificance against more Mystery Marble Sender news. We found another marble at the zoo! And there's something about Mystery Marble Sender's note . . . the list of shopping errands on the end . . . that has tickled my memory. The yellow jacket—it's something to do with a yellow jacket. And warts. . . I can almost see someone wearing a yellow jacket and tackling their fungal feet . . . but who? Is it my destiny to find out?

Hmmm . . . destiny . . . Wait. Shhhh! What was that?

Who's there? Josh? Danny?

What?! Hey! What do you think you're—

NO! DOOF! GAH!

Eeeeeeeeeeeeeeeek.

CRSSHHSZZZZ—kesheeek—ssheeeek—sheeeek.

Ssssssssssssssssssssssssssssssssssssssssssss
ssssssssssssssssssssssssssssssssssssssssssss
ssssssssssssssssssssssssssssssssssssssssssss
ssssssssssssssssssssssssssssssssssssssssssss
ssssssssssssss

"What does 'CRSSHHSZZZZ—kesheeek—ssheeeek—sheeeek' mean?" Danny murmured.

"Nothing good," Josh said.

"Maybe we should just tell Mom and Dad everything when they get back from shopping," sighed Danny.

"But they'll never believe us, either!" Josh said.

"Not all the stuff about her S.W.I.T.C.H.ing us into spiders and frogs and snakes and stuff. Just that we think she's in trouble," Danny said.

"And then what?" Josh asked. "They'll call the police who will break into her house—*boom*— *crash*—*fizz*—mangled people! If only Petty wasn't so paranoid about people being out to get her!"

"Yeah," Danny said. "But it looks like someone *did* get her."

Josh and Danny frowned at each other over Piddle's head. They were thinking of the same thing. The Mystery Marble Sender. The person who had been messing with their minds for weeks now, sending clues to get them to find marbles . . . but not just any marbles.

"We knew something *big* was going to happen next, after we got that fifth marble," Josh said. "We knew there was only one more to go. And that the Mystery Marble Sender would soon do something. Because there was no way he was just giving us clues to find all the marbles, with the secret code to MAMMALSWITCH formula, free. He wants something. And I think it's Petty—or what's in Petty's genius head."

"Well, if she's been kidnapped," Danny said, "I think *we* might get the ransom note. Probably quite soon . . . I mean, there's nobody else to send it to, is there? She's got no family."

Piddle suddenly got up and tore out of the den, yapping loudly. He ran down the side passage and around to the front of the house. This usually meant somebody was coming in through the gate. Josh and Danny, still worried and gloomy, scrambled out of the bush and went down the side passage to see who was there.

They saw nobody at the gate or the front door— or anywhere around the garden. But Piddle was still flinging himself against the garden wall. Mom and Dad had arrived, though. Dad was in the kitchen, sorting out the groceries, and Mom was watching Chatz TV. The sound of the show drifted through the front room window. Mom and Jenny liked to watch it most afternoons, although Josh and Danny couldn't imagine *why*. It was mostly people shouting angrily at each other in front of a studio audience. Still, Mom was watching it now and obviously hadn't been interrupted by anyone at the door.

"Shut up, Piddle!" Danny called, and the little dog gave one last disgruntled *wuff* and then ran back down the side passage. Josh stood very still. Across the low wall, he could just make out somebody standing silently on Petty's front step.

"Come on," he said, grabbing Danny's arm and leading him round to Petty's. A dark-haired young woman in a grey suit stood with her back to the door, holding a briefcase. She clearly did not expect anyone to open the door. She smiled tightly at them as they walked up the path.

"You must be Josh and Danny Phillips," she said. "I've been waiting for you."

Brief Encounter

The young woman opened her case and took out a brown envelope. "I am Petty Potts's lawyer," she said, in a businesslike voice. "And it is incumbent upon me to place this directly into your hands herewith."

"You what?" Danny said.

The lawyer sighed and checked her watch. "It was my client's instruction that nobody else should see this," she said, waving the brown envelope, "and that it should be handed directly to you two and nobody else. That's why I've had to stand around in this doorway waiting for you to come along."

"It's a letter for us?" Danny queried.

"The clue is on the envelope!" snapped the lawyer.

"No need to be snarky," Josh said, taking it from her. "When did Petty ask you to give us this?"

"She didn't ask me," the lawyer said, closing her case with a click. "She left me instructions many weeks ago to deliver this to you two if she ever failed to call me and check in. Most weeks she makes a phone call on a certain day and gives me a code word, so I know all is well. If she doesn't make that call, I have to wait forty-eight hours . . . and then deliver this to you. Well . . . she hasn't called, it's been forty-eight hours . . . and here I am. Now, if you don't mind, I must be on my way to another client. Good-bye." Her heels clicked away down the sidewalk, and then she was out of sight.

Josh and Danny stared at each other across the brown envelope. Josh tore it open. Inside was a piece of lined paper. He expected a letter—some explanation, maybe, about where she'd gone and why. But it wasn't a letter. It was a list in Petty's scrawly handwriting.

He and Danny sat down on Petty's tiled doorstep to peer at the list.

1. DADDY LONGLEGS DISCO—COLLECT.
2. IF UNSEEN, ENTER.
3. DUCK. FAST.
4. WALK THE STAINS.
5. AFTER THIRD STRIKE, DO NOT BREATHE UNTIL THE BIRD CALLS.
6. WASH UP. USE GLOVES.
7. EXIT BACK ON ALL FOURS.
8. ONE MINUTE FROM RED DOOR.
9. WORKING LUNCH.
10. ONE MINUTE FROM RED DOOR!

"What on earth does all that mean?" squawked Danny.

Josh was creasing his brow trying to figure it out. "It's instructions. Something we have to do."

"Walk the stains?" Danny said. "Daddy
Longlegs Disco? She's lost it. Completely. I mean,
we always knew she was bonkers, but now she's
totally gaga!"

"No." Josh smoothed the paper out on the
step. "There's logic to it. It's like crossword clues.
We have to get one or two of them and then the
others will start to make sense."

"OK," Danny said with a shrug. "Let's start
with Number One . . . Daddy Longlegs Disco . . ."

Josh puzzled. Danny puzzled too. They flopped
down on Petty's doorstep with big sighs. It had
been a freaky enough day already without having
to figure out cryptic clues!

Then Josh's eyes widened, and he gave a shout.
"Whoa! Wait! This is EASY!"

"What?" Danny sat up straight.

"Daddy Longlegs Disco!" Josh said. "Don't
you remember? When we were daddy longlegs,
we went out, didn't we? We flew toward the
light where loads of other creepy-crawlies were
boogying about and head-butting the bulb."

"Yeah—that hurt," remembered Danny. Josh

was looking up. Right *up* above them. At the little square porch light over their heads. "It's where we found a REPTOSWITCH cube, isn't it?" Danny jumped to his feet. "She's hidden something else in there! Quick—help me up!"

Checking first that nobody was watching, Josh hoisted Danny up on his shoulders. "Eeeeeugh!" he heard Danny call down. "There're dead things in here!"

"Don't be a wuss!" hissed Josh. "Find the thing . . . whatever it is. Quickly. You're breaking my neck!"

Danny made a few more whimpers as some disembodied legs and wings floated down. But then he whispered, "*Got it!*" He jumped off his brother's shoulders and waved a door key.

"Right," Josh said, consulting the list. "Number Two. 'If unseen, enter.'"

Danny looked around again and then shoved the key into the lock of Petty's front door. It turned easily.

"Hang on," Josh said.

Danny pushed the door open.

"Wait a bit," Josh said, grabbing his arm. But Danny had already stepped through.

"DUCK!" screamed Josh! "FAST!"

Danny hit the floor. Josh followed . . . a little too late.

There was a sudden thump of air and a powerful roar.

A ball of flame was flying toward them.

The Washing-Up of Death

They didn't have time to scream. Flames filled the doorway. Facedown on the welcome mat, Danny felt the heat blast across his shoulders. Josh felt the heat too . . . in his hair.

The flame was there and gone in seconds. Except for the bit in Josh's hair. Little flickers of flame were dancing through his short blonde crop. Danny threw himself at Josh's head and batted the flames out.

Then they sat very still on the doormat and stared at each other. Josh's hair was singed. It smelled awful. But the flames had not reached his skin. In fact, the ball of fire had done very little damage to the hallway. It had obviously been designed to fly directly through the front door at around chest height. If they had not ducked— fast—they would have been barbecued.

"Petty's security system!" whispered Josh. "We DO NOT MOVE . . . not until we've figured out the next two or three instructions!"

Danny nodded, carefully closing the front door so they could sit and think without being seen.

"Number Four," Josh said, in a slightly shaky voice. "Walk the stains."

They looked around them. "Walk the stains," murmured Danny. "Erm . . . do you think she means those stains?" He pointed across the hallway carpet. It was a very old carpet that had once been a cream color. There were lots of stains on it, but Danny saw that some were more noticeable than others—five or six darker ones leading down the hall like stepping stones.

"The brown ones?" Josh said.

"Yeah . . . chocolate cake stains," Danny said. "Petty's always eating chocolate cake . . . I think she's dropped some chocolate icing deliberately— to mark a path . . ."

"So . . ." Josh pondered. "If we walk on those chocolate cake stains, it should be a safe path through to . . . the kitchen, by the looks of it.

Because Number Six is 'Wash up. Use gloves.'"

"OK," Danny got up and went to step out.

"Wait!" Josh grabbed his arm. "We need to be sure of what's coming next! Number Five is this: 'After third strike, DO NOT BREATHE until the bird calls.'"

They screwed up their faces again, trying to figure this one out. "What bird?" Danny said. "I can't see a bird anywhere."

"OK," Josh said. "Let's just walk the stains first—see how that goes."

Danny stepped across to the first dark splodge. His foot landed on it. He froze, waiting for something terrible to happen. Nothing did. He shrugged and stepped to the next splodge. Josh followed his path. Danny could feel his heart thumping hard in his chest. He knew that, at any moment, something extremely violent could happen. Petty left nothing to chance. Outside, the sun went behind a cloud, and the hallway grew dimmer.

"Josh! Look!" Danny froze and carefully pointed to his right. In the dimness, he could see a needle of blue light shining down from the ceiling. And now Josh could see several more of them—piercing though the dark of the hallway at different angles.

"Lasers!" breathed Danny. "If we hit one of those . . ." He gulped. He had no idea what would happen if they hit a laser beam—but he knew it would be nasty.

"We won't hit one," Josh said. "Not if we follow the cake stains!"

It seemed Josh was right. A minute later, they were safely by the kitchen door. And that's when they heard a chime. Two chimes. Three.

"HOLD YOUR BREATH!" squeaked Josh, remembering Number Five—"*After third strike, DO NOT BREATHE until the bird calls.*" With half a second to spare, he and Danny dragged in a swift lungful of air and held it, their eyes bulging with anxiety.

On the fourth strike, there was a loud hiss, and two plumes of purple gas suddenly punched out of the wall on either side of the door. Danny could feel it stinging his eyes. He screwed them shut, desperate to hold onto the safe air in his lungs for as long as possible. The clock chimed on from the other side of the closed kitchen door—five . . . six . . . seven . . . Danny felt as if his lungs were going to burst. Eight . . . nine . . . ten . . . . Josh was twisting around, desperate to see some kind of bird somewhere through the fading purple gas. Eleven . . . twelve . . . thirteen. *THIRTEEN?* Danny felt his mind flip. Had he lost count? Or was the clock really striking thirteen? Fourteen, fifteen, sixteen, seventeen . . . . Josh felt faint. He must breathe soon! But no bird had called. And the air might still be poisoned! *Eighteen . . . nineteen . . . .*

CUCKOO! CUCKOO! CUCKOO!

Danny and Josh exploded with exhaled air and pushed through the kitchen door, gasping. On

the wall was a cuckoo clock, from which a little wooden bird was calling.

At last the cuckooing stopped. Josh and Danny stood, panting and shaking, ready for their next instruction.

"*Wash up*," puffed Josh. The washing-up bowl was full of cold water and crockery. Little bits of orangey grease and lumps of unidentifiable food floated across the surface, along with a semi-submerged scrubby sponge thing.

Danny stepped over and went to pick up the scrubby sponge thing.

"STOP!" Josh yelled. "*USE GLOVES!*" Danny paused. He grabbed a pair of limp yellow rubber gloves from the draining board.

"There's no telling what Petty put in that washing bowl," muttered Josh. "Skin-melting acid, I bet. Or a deadly virus!"

Danny didn't wash up. He took all the cups and bowls and spoons and forks out of the water. He laid them down in a scummy puddle on the draining board. He looked for something hidden underneath them. "Bingo!" he said, lifting up another key.

"I've seen this before," said Josh, taking the key as Danny carefully peeled off the gloves. "It's the key to Petty's shed . . . and her old laboratory." He gulped. "The next instruction is 'Exit back on all fours.'"

Quickly, they unbolted the back door and crawled across the threshold. Two inches above Josh's burnt hair, three arrows shot across from one side of the doorway, embedding themselves in the wooden frame. A foul-smelling liquid oozed from the wounds they made in the paintwork. "Poison tipped," whispered Danny with a gulp.

It was a relief to be in the back garden. The weeds grew above their heads, so they bashed a path through to the shed without any fear of being seen

from nearby houses. The key fit into the padlock on the shed. In a few seconds, they were inside. They passed the neglected old lawnmower, the pointless wheelbarrow, and the never-used rake. They stopped at the hidden door at the back of the shed.

It felt very odd to go down into Petty's old underground lab, knowing that she was not in it. It had always smelled pretty weird. But now it also smelled neglected and damp.

Josh found a switch on the wall just inside the door. He switched it on. Light flooded through the room. It had once been filled with Petty's stuff, but now it was empty apart from some trestle

tables, shelves, and boxes. In a booth in the corner was a very old computer. Petty had new ones at the new lab, and this one now looked ready for the trash heap.

"Eeerm . . . how long have we been in here?" Josh asked, suddenly sounding panicky.

"Dunno," Danny said, staring around at the forlorn ex-lab.

"Because . . . Number Eight says, "'One minute from red door.'" And I don't like the sound of that."

Nor did Danny. He checked his watch. "Maybe thirty seconds?" he guessed. "What's Number Nine?"

"Working lunch," whispered Josh, his eyes wide and fearful as he checked his own watch. "Ten seconds to work that out, I think!"

"There's no work going on here!" whimpered Danny. "Nothing! Except . . . wait!" He ran toward the little booth with its ancient computer.

"Danny—we've got to get out!" said Josh. He could feel something rumbling under his feet.

"I think this could be it!" Danny had found a lunchbox by the computer in the booth—which was shaking. Quite a lot.

"DANNY! COME OUT NOW!" yelled Josh. "Something's happening! Something BAD!"

Danny could feel that for himself. The rumbling was getting louder. And there was a hissing and screeching noise joining it. The ground was trembling under his feet.

"COME ON! RUN!" shrieked Josh, hanging on to the doorway as the whole room began to sway.

Danny wanted to run. But it wasn't easy. A huge crack had just opened up across the center of the floor.

From the Beyond

The crack tore itself open right in front of Danny's eyes. The earth beneath it seemed to dissolve away. A red glow and a gassy smell rose up from it. Then suddenly—flames leapt up! Danny shrieked. Josh bellowed, "JUUUUUMP! Jump NOW! Before it's TOO LATE!!"

Danny was on a little shelf of ground with the computer booth just behind him. The shelf was beginning to crumble away. Incredibly, Petty had built some kind of collapsing pit over a gas fire trap! He had to jump now, or there would be nothing left to jump from. Below him, in the widening chasm, there were hissing and grinding and whining noises. Flames were shooting up higher. He shoved the lunchbox down his shirt, coughing as the gas caught in his throat. It was now or never. Danny jumped.

He leapt across the fire pit, his arms waving frantically through the air. He crashed into the rough edge of the crumbling floor. He would have slipped into the pit if Josh hadn't grabbed his wrists and pulled him up. "Come on!" screamed Josh. He looked terrified. And he had every reason to be. The whole room was breaking apart. The old corrugated iron ceiling was shaking and buckling. Dirt and grit cascaded down. As Josh and Danny scrambled back up the tunnel toward the shed, there was a huge *WHUMP* behind them. Glancing back, they saw the roof fall in. Dirt, grit, roots, and old brick tumbled into the flaming pit. Josh and Danny flung themselves through the metal door to the shed, across the wooden floor, and out into the garden. They landed in the tall weeds just as the shed collapsed. It tilted over toward the back and then just fell apart as if it were made of playing cards. The mower and the wheelbarrow stayed put on the floor. The wooden walls and the roof slithered to the ground. Rakes, hoes, and spades tumbled with it. Plastic plant pots bounced across the wreckage.

Then . . . silence. In the garden, all evidence of what had just happened seemed to evaporate along with a cloud of dust. After a minute, the birds started singing again. Josh and Danny walked carefully across to the shed and peered at the back, where the doorway and the tunnel had once been. Tugging up the collapsed wooden panels, they found the back wall and the red door lying flat. And when they pulled the door up, they found nothing but dirt and grit and rubble beneath it. No sign of any secret passage to an underground lab. Nothing.

"Petty set it to self-destruct," marveled Josh. "So if anyone went in for longer than a minute . . . *boom!* Everything gone."

"Not everything," Danny said. And he pulled a small metal lunchbox out of his shirt. Sitting down in the tall weeds, they carefully opened it. Inside, set tightly into black foam, were twenty-one small plastic spray bottles, each about the size of a cotton reel. There was a label on each. The first label read "SPIDER." The seventh label read "FROG." The twenty-first label read "ALLIGATOR."

"Wow!" Danny stared at Josh in amazement. "It's the complete set of Petty's S.W.I.T.C.H. sprays! Every single one!"

"And you think she left them for us?" queried Josh.

"Well—let's find out!" Danny said, and he pulled out a slim, silver gadget from the box. There was a label on it that read "PLAY ME." It was a digital recording device. Danny pressed PLAY, and a familiar voice rang out.

"Aaahh! If that's Josh and Danny listening—well done! And if it's not Josh and Danny, bad luck. This device is set to explode if it picks up traces of DNA from anyone else. So . . . three . . . two . . . one . . . BYEEEEEE."

Josh and Danny edged back from the box.

"But if I'm still talking, it is you, Josh and Danny. Good work, boys! Good work. I hope you didn't find the self-destruct system in the lab too troublesome. Rest assured that there is nothing left down there now except rubble and mud. No possible way for Victor Crouch to find any trace of my S.W.I.T.C.H. project. Now—in the box is a complete set of all the sprays I have made so far. And if you've got them, it must mean that I have gone missing, presumed dead. Yes . . . I'm most likely dead."

Josh and Danny grimaced at each other.

"And oh—what a loss to science!" lamented the voice. "How utterly, utterly terrible! But you—Josh and Danny—you must carry on my work!"

"Us?" Danny looked appalled. "We're not genius scientists! We're eight!"

"Now don't start getting all spluttery, Danny," went on Petty, as if she was right there with them. "And Josh—you will need your sensible head on. Contact the editor of *New Scientist* magazine and tell him everything! I want the whole world to know what a genius I am. Or was. Oh . . . ." Petty had a little sniff. "*What* a loss . . . *what* a terrible loss . . . ."

There was a click and the recording ended.

Danny and Josh sat in silence for a few seconds.

"Do you think she's really dead?" asked Danny, after a while.

Josh shook his head. "No. I don't think so. Someone kidnapped her. And we still have to find her."

"But now," Danny said, a grin spreading across his grimy face, "we've got something to help!" He tapped the box of S.W.I.T.C.H. sprays. "We can be anything from a bluebottle to an alligator!"

"Yes," Josh said. "And how does that help, exactly?"

"Erm . . ." Danny said.

It was one thing to have Petty's complete set of S.W.I.T.C.H. sprays. It was quite another to know what to do with them.

They got up and trudged down the garden, to the loose plank in the fence at the far end. They did not plan to retrace their steps through the deadly house. Back in their own garden they headed indoors and hid the lunchbox of S.W.I.T.C.H. sprays under the bunk bed. Mom was appalled when she saw the state of them. And Josh's singed hair took some explaining. Josh had to say he'd been playing with matches. He lost a week's worth of allowance.

After a bath, they really could not think of anything else to do except watch TV in a daze . . .

which wasn't a great idea, because that dreadful
Destiny Darcy show was on. "Don't forget,
people!" she was simpering into the camera.
"We're on tour! Coming to a town near you!
Come and meet Destiny!"

Josh and Danny groaned and went to bed.

Pretty Potts

Petty Potts sat back in the chair. A young lady was patting something slightly damp on her face. Petty hadn't a clue what . . . or why . . . or where she was.

"Hmmmm," pondered the young lady. "You're an Extra Fair foundation. Don't want to make you too orange. It doesn't look good on camera. Now . . . Mulberry lipstick, I think. Just relax your mouth . . . there! Lovely!"

Petty stared blearily into the mirror with light bulbs all round it. She was wearing makeup. Makeup! She *never* wore makeup!

"Hair looks great!" said the young lady, who wore an apron and a great deal of purple lip gloss. She had many palettes of color spread out on the table under the mirror, along with pots and brushes and pencils.

Petty squinted at her hair.

"Here—put your glasses back on," said the young lady. She handed Petty a pair of unusually clean glasses. Petty put them on and stared into the mirror. Her hair was still gray but no longer straggly and wild. It was neatly trimmed and styled—and she appeared to be wearing a *dress*.

"Good grief!" muttered Petty.

"Well—we all have to make an effort for Destiny Darcy, don't we?" said the young lady chirpily. "OK—if you can go back to the green room now, I can get on and do KettleMan."

"The green room?" queried Petty. She glanced across at the man seated next to her, who had a silver kettle fixed firmly to his head.

"Yes—where you'll be waiting," said the young lady. "You know . . . before you go on?"

"Go on what?!" demanded Petty.

"On TV, of course!"

Make it Snappy

Danny stared at the little white spray bottle in his hand. There was no doubt about it. The label read "Alligator." He was one squirt away from turning into one of the world's most powerful, terrifying reptiles.

Josh stared at it too. His eyes shone. Danny knew Josh was thinking exactly what he was thinking.

"Mom and Dad are out," he said. "Jenny's upstairs watching that stupid Darcy show in her bedroom. She *never* comes into the garden anyway. Nobody will ever know."

Josh nodded slowly. In the shady bush den, he shivered with excitement. They'd spent most of the morning wondering what to do about Petty and coming up with exactly nothing. There was *no way* they were going to get the police—or, *worse,* their parents—to start searching for Petty. Because they knew the very first thing anyone would do would be to break into her house . . . and then they'd probably end up flash-fried or gassed or poisoned by arrows or deadly dishwater. They should be able to come up with a master plan, but so far they hadn't come up with one.

And in the meantime . . .

"Come on!" Danny said. "You know you want to!"

"OK," said Josh. "A tiny squirt—so we can S.W.I.T.C.H. for just a few minutes. See what it's like. We can stay down at the end of the garden where we won't be seen."

Danny lost no time. He squirted Josh first, and then himself. He shoved the bottle quickly back into his jeans pocket before he could S.W.I.T.C.H.

Josh felt peculiar for just a few seconds, and then—*WHOOOMP!* All of a sudden, he was flat on his belly, crouching low to the ground. He could feel the weight and strength of his new body. And he could see his broad snout stretching

out and tapering to a blunted end with two high
nostrils. He gave a hiss of delight. This was the
most amazing thing he had ever been. He turned
around on his thick, muscular legs, noticing the
way the five-clawed toes on his forelegs dug deep
into the soil under the bushes. His tail—three feet
long—swished around behind him and hit some
of the straggly trunks of the rhododendron with
a crack. He grinned. He could feel the immense
power in his muscles—it tingled along his tail
and up the five rows of dark brown, spiny ridges
running up his back to his neck.

Another alligator was grinning back at him. "This is the *best ever*!" Danny said, his voice coming out as a low grunt.

"American Alligator!" grunted back Josh, with glee. "*Mississippiensis*!"

"You what?" Danny said, leaving his enormous snaggle-toothed jaws open and tilting his heavy head to one side.

"It's the Latin name," Josh said. "For some reason, I remember it. *Mississippiensis*! I guess they must be found in the Mississippi River."

"Look at my tail!" marveled Danny, turning his dark brown, scaly head to stare down the length of his body. "We're *huge*! How long, do you reckon?"

"About ten feet," guessed Josh. "Alligators can be nearly twice as big this! We're small fry!"

"And what do we eat?" asked Danny.

"Anything we like!" Josh let out a chuckle, which came out as a series of grunts and hisses.

"How are we talking?" asked Danny.

"Not the usual way," Josh said. "We don't have any vocal cords. We just use the air in our bodies to sort of grunt and hiss and bellow. But it's the other ways too—you know, scent, body language, animal telepathy—that kind of thing."

"Come on!" hissed Danny. "Let's take a walk!" He rose up a little on his stumpy legs and walked across the lawn to the jungle gym and back again. His body and tail swung from side to side, low to the ground. "I feel heavy!" he said.

"You are heavy!" Josh said. "You're designed to be in water. We must get down to the lake in the park and S.W.I.T.C.H. there. That would be *amazing*!"

"I'm hungry," Danny said. "Really hungry!" He could hear lively yapping. Piddle was scratching at the kitchen door. "Hey—check out my teeth!" He opened his jaws, revealing about eighty sharp teeth.

"When they fall out, new ones grow in in their place," Josh said. "Alligators can go through three thousand teeth in a lifetime. Imagine that!"

There was a sudden rattle down inside the passage—the sound of the kitchen door being opened. Josh and Danny stared at each other, alarmed. They heard the voice of their big sister.

"Get out, you disgusting little pee bag!" Jenny was shoving their dog outside. "Go and do your business outside! All I want to do is watch *Destiny Darcy* and you have to come along and pee on my feet!"

And then Piddle came trotting into the back garden. When he saw Josh and Danny, he froze, and all the hair on his body stood up.

"Piddle! It's OK!" hissed Danny. "It's us!"

Piddle whimpered and backed away, terrified.

"Really—it's just us," went on Danny,

lumbering toward Piddle. "Danny and Josh!"

Piddle backed right into a corner by the shed, growling and shivering. "You don't have to be afraid!" insisted Danny. And then he opened his immense jaws . . .

And closed them on Piddle.

Getting in Tents

"DANNY! STOP! STOP!" Josh bellowed.

"Whaaa-at? I'm only playing!" Danny said.
He turned around and grinned at Josh. Piddle,
jammed in Danny's teeth, squirmed and yelped.

"STOP IT! You might eat him by mistake!" Josh
whacked Danny hard with his powerful tail. Piddle
shot out of Danny's jaws and landed in a soggy
lump right in front of Josh.

Josh had to admit that the urge to snap up the
little dog was very strong. Poor Piddle lay in a
puddle, staring up at Josh in horror. But to Josh,
he smelled a lot like dinner. Josh realized his jaws
had opened. Very wide . . . .

Which was why it was a very good thing that
he S.W.I.T.C.H.ed back right at that moment. He
found Piddle's tail in his mouth, even so.

"Sorry—*sorry*!" He grabbed the shocked pet and rubbed his head. Over by the shed, Danny was also back in boy shape and looking rather ashamed. He came over to say sorry to Piddle too. But Piddle just wriggled out of Josh's grasp and bolted away through the side yard.

"That was a bit . . . bad," muttered Josh. "We've never tried to eat Piddle before."

"No," agreed Danny. He shrugged. "But he's tried to eat *us*. Several times. So I think we're even."

Josh still felt bad, even though Piddle *had* nearly eaten him when he was a daddy longlegs—and had actually chewed on Danny when Danny was a frog.

"Come on," he said. "Let's go down to the park and try to AlligatorS.W.I.T.C.H. in the lake."

"What if we get seen, though?" asked Danny. It was Saturday, and he knew the park would be busy. "And what if we get munchy around some person's dog. . . ?"

"Or some dog's person . . ." said Josh darkly. He sighed. He was still very shaken up by nearly eating Piddle. "Maybe we should just stay here. Think harder about what we're going to do about Petty."

"Yes," said Danny. "We shouldn't really be having fun while she's in some kidnapper's den." He shook his head. "There could be torture. Screaming, yelling, slapping, shouting in the face . . . . I bet they won't keep her for long once she starts all that."

They went back indoors and hid the lunchbox deep under the bunk bed. Then they sat on the floor, trying to think. After a few minutes of this, Jenny barged into the room and chucked something at them. "Just came in the mail," she muttered. "Can't think why anyone bothers to send stuff to you two dweebs!" And she turned and went out again.

Danny picked up a yellow envelope with their names on it. He ripped it open while Josh leaned

over his shoulder. This could be it . . . a message from the kidnapper.

Inside, though, was a printed invitation. It read:

DESTINY IN THE PARK!

Don't miss the *Destiny Darcy Show*, recording at
YOUR LOCAL PARK this Saturday at noon!

"That's today!' said Josh, peering at the glossy photo of Destiny Darcy in front of a live studio audience. "In about an hour! It's a bit late to send an invitation out to everyone, isn't it?"

"But I don't think this *has* been sent to everyone," Danny said. He flipped the card over, and on the back was some familiar scrawly writing.

COME ALONG, JOSH AND DANNY. IT'S TIME TO MEET DESTINY. AND SEE YOUR MARBLE MAKER AGAIN!

Josh and Danny stared at each other. Destiny? *Their* destiny? Or . . . Destiny Darcy?

"Come on!" Danny said, jumping to his feet.

"The marbles and Petty's kidnapping—it's all tied up with Destiny! Destiny Darcy!"

"Wait," Josh said, grabbing the lunchbox back out from under the bed. "We're going prepared!"

The park was busier than usual. There were big trucks and a couple of large yellow tents set up by the lake. There was a large, metal dish thing set up on one of the trucks.

"It's a TV show all right," Danny said. "Look—they've got cameras and an audience and stuff." Audience clapping and cheering and whooping could be heard from inside the larger tent.

Josh screwed up his face when he saw what was written on the tent in huge black letters. "I can't believe we're going to see the *DESTINY DARCY SHOW*! It's the one Mom and Jenny are so nuts about. It's awful!"

"But it all connects with the Mystery Marble Sender and Petty," Josh said. "So we *have* to go in."

Danny suddenly stood still, clutching the yellow envelope.

"Let's go in," Josh said. "Or we might never see Petty again."

They gazed at the big yellow tent for a few seconds. Then they walked toward it.

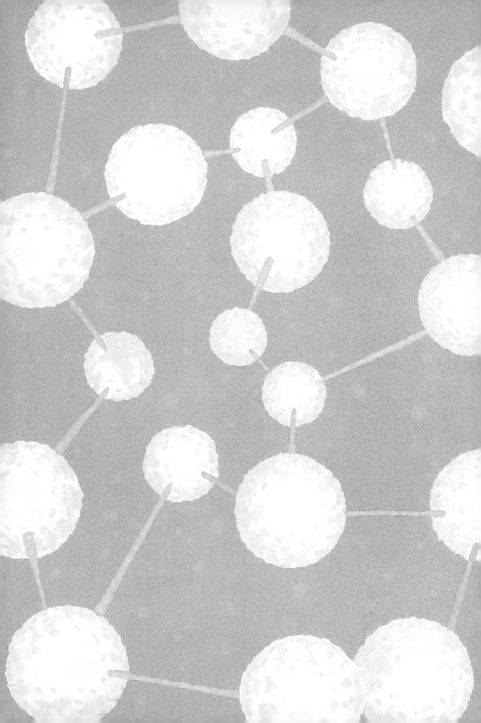

Dreamy. Steamy. Screamy.

Petty started to fully wake up just at the point
when she was led into the wings of the stage.
The last few hours had seemed like some weird
dream . . . but then she could hear the rowdy
audience, and she knew it was real. The audience
was shouting at the man with the kettle on his
head. There was a short, plump, red-haired woman
sitting next to him on the sofa, crying into a
wadded-up tissue.

"I just don't understand it," sniffed the woman.
"I sent him to a nice school. Cooked his favorite
dinners. Let him watch all his favorite TV shows.
Bought him lots of toys. And for what? For him to
grow up pretending to be a superhero with a kettle
on his head!"

The kettle-headed man sprang to his feet

and shouted, "I am NOT pretending to be a superhero, Mother. I AM a superhero!"

The audience laughed and booed. Then a dark-haired woman in a sparkly yellow jacket shimmied across the stage with a microphone. "Well, Brian," she asked, "If you are a superhero, what are your super powers? What can KettleMan do? Apart from make lots of really hot cups of tea . . ."

The audience fell apart, exploding in laughter. KettleMan was now steaming. Literally. He pressed a switch on the kettle on his head, and a jet of steam shot out of the long spout above his eyebrows. "BEHOLD MY POWER!" he shouted. Then two burly security guards grabbed him and dragged him offstage. "If I WANT to be

KettleMan, I have the RIGHT to be KettleMan!"
shouted Brian as he was dragged past Petty. His
mother hurried after him, looking weary.

Destiny Darcy sighed, gazed at the audience,
and said, "So sad!"

She walked to the center of the stage and
stared out into the crowd. There were about two
hundred people squeezed into the tent. They
perched on tiered seating, which had been set up
on some kind of scaffolding. They were behaving
every bit as badly as they would in the proper TV
studio back in London, thought Destiny. It was a
good idea to take the show on tour. A *very* good
idea. And now, it was going to get even better.

"Imagine how it feels," Destiny said, her voice
a whisper, echoing through the many speakers
in the tent, "to know that your mother rejected
you." The audience made a sympathetic murmur.
"To know that her work was always *far* more
important than her daughter." Destiny's voice
began to rise. "To realize that she was SO
selfishly caught up in her own ambition that
she—LITERALLY—forgot you existed!"

Standing in the wings, Petty Potts felt her arm being taken by one of the burly security men. "I'm NOT going out there!" she exclaimed.

"Oh, yes, you are, love!" he replied, gripping her arm tighter. "This is Chatz TV's biggest show. Nobody walks out on it."

Petty stamped on his foot. But he didn't seem to notice. Back onstage, Destiny Darcy was still talking. Goose pimples ran up and down Petty's spine. There was something weirdly familiar about that voice . . . .

"Today, I bring you a world exclusive," Destiny said. "A story which will shock you to the core. Because the coldhearted, ruthlessly ambitious mother who neglected her own daughter is HERE TODAY! Bring her on, boys!"

And Petty was propelled into the hot, bright stage lights to a chorus of boos and catcalls.

"And the daughter she FORGOT . . ." went on Destiny, turning to stare at Petty.

". . . is **ME!**"

The audience gasped. Josh and Danny were so shocked they just sat in their seats, mouths open.

Petty Potts had a DAUGHTER?

Back onstage, sinking into the leather sofa, was Petty, peering at Destiny Darcy in absolute amazement.

"What are you talking about, you deranged woman?" she spluttered. "I haven't got a daughter!"

"Oh no?" Destiny said. "Then I wonder who this is."

Up on a big, white screen at the back of the
stage, a photo appeared. Josh's and Danny's
mouths dropped open even wider. It was the photo
from Petty's new lab. They'd just seen it days ago.
It was of Petty's former best friend—and now
worst enemy—Victor Crouch, with his arm around
Petty. And next to Petty on the other side was a
teenage girl who was undoubtedly Destiny Darcy.

There was a gasp of amazement from
the audience.

"That's the bit of the photo that was cut out
of the frame!" hissed Danny, finding his voice at
last. "We thought it looked odd!"

Petty was gaping too now. *That girl in the photo DOES look familiar,* she thought. *Didn't Victor Crouch give me the same photo years ago? If so . . . why was the girl cut off the end of my copy?* So I would forget she existed? "This is ludicrous!" she muttered, aloud. "How could I forget having my *own* daughter?"

She shook her head. As she did so, some of the more recent memories slid back the right way up. She suddenly recalled being kidnapped from her lab only days before. She shook her head again, trying to remember who'd kidnapped her.

Destiny Darcy saw the head-shaking and began to stomp around the stage in a rage, her black sequined trousers glittering and flouncing in the TV lights. "You STILL don't believe me?" she shouted. "Well—how about this for proof?" She held up a bit of paper with the words POSITIVE MATCH written on it in large blue letters. A cameraman whizzed up to her, focusing on the paper. Behind her, the huge screen above the stage cut to the image. It said "DNA TEST" at the top.

"I have PROOF!" snarled Destiny. "I know how to prove who is related to who!"

"Whom," Petty said. "Who is related to *whom.* Surely if I was really your mother, you would have learned better grammar."

"GAAAH!" shouted Destiny, stamping her foot. "You were ALWAYS just like this!"

Petty sat still and tried to work out what to do next. All she really wanted to do was to get back to her lab and find Josh and Danny and carry on with the S.W.I.T.C.H. project.

"And what hurts most of ALL . . ." Destiny furiously paced the stage as the audience sat transfixed. ". . . is exactly WHAT all that research you were doing—the research that meant you FORGOT I EXISTED—was FOR!"

Suddenly, she took a small drawstring bag out of her jacket pocket. "THIS," she told the audience, "is my mother's GREAT WORK!" She tipped up the bag, and marbles rained out of it and clacked onto the stage, rolling off in all directions.

"Yes," said Destiny. "My mother has spent

her ENTIRE LIFE working on a new design . . . for MARBLES!"

The audience gasped, then laughed and jeered.

Josh and Danny stared at each other, feeling panicky. "It's definitely *her*!" hissed Danny. "Destiny Darcy is the Mystery Marble Sender!" And now, of course, it began to fall into place, thought Josh! The black sequin in the note, the prize from Chatz TV containing one of the marbles—there were even Destiny Darcy Diddly DeeDee dolls in the goody bags where they'd found their last marble.

"The *Destiny Darcy Show* was in Cornwall, when we got the third marble!" hissed Danny. "Jenny and her friend went to it, remember?"

"And there was a Chatz TV tent up at the zoo when we S.W.I.T.C.H.ed into anacondas!" remembered Josh.

Back onstage, scrabbling to pick up the marbles, Petty was furious. "You FOOLISH woman," she shouted. "You have NO IDEA what these are, have you?"

"Well," smirked Destiny, "whatever you think they are, Mother, you've obviously LOST YOUR MARBLES!"

The audience hooted.

"But this is sad," Destiny said, her face suddenly tragic. "Because, clearly, my mother has gone insane. And earlier today, a good friend of hers and I . . . well . . . this is terribly hard to say, but we signed the forms to have her committed . . . to a mental asylum!"

Petty, with her hands full of marbles, was alert and staring around. "Look," she said. "Destiny . . . Maybe I do remember you after all!"

"Oh-ho!" chortled Destiny, "And now perhaps you conveniently remember this man too!"

And then, to the tune of a theme song, a man walked onstage. He carried a hat and had a full head of light brown hair, which was obviously a wig. His eyebrows had been penciled in, but Josh and Danny could still see the long, sharpened fingernail on the little finger of his left hand. And even if they hadn't seen it, they knew.

"It's *him*!" hissed Josh, shocked and scared.

"Ladies and gentlemen," sang out Destiny Darcy as the man took his place next to Petty on the sofa. "This is my godfather and my mother's oldest friend—VICTOR CROUCH!"

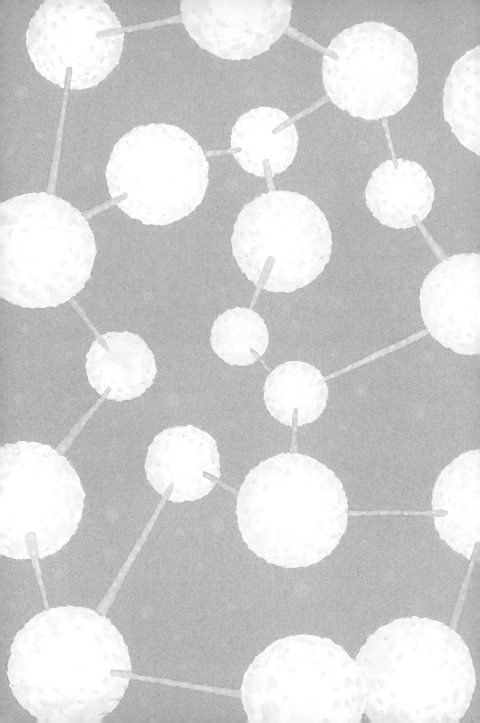

Men in White Coats

Victor Crouch smiled sadly at Petty and attempted to pat her shoulder as she stood up, leaving the marbles to roll across the stage. Petty slapped his hand away. He sighed and turned his hurt face to the audience.

"It is a terribly tragic case," he said. "I was Petty's best friend for many years."

"Aaaaaaah," went the audience.

"Yes! Until you decided to stab me in the back, steal my work, and burn my memory out!" raged Petty. "Some kind of friend you turned out to be!"

"Aaaaaaaw!" went the audience.

"Ah, Petty," sighed Victor Crouch, "it is very sad that you can't remember what *really* happened. You worked far too hard, and your mind just snapped . . . Poor Destiny and I tried to help, but you were really quite mad by then, and you pretended you didn't even know us. It broke poor Destiny's heart . . ."

Petty's face twitched as she stared at Destiny. "Do something for me," she asked the chat show host. "Take off your shoes!"

Destiny looked confused. "Take off my shoes?"

"Yes, dear. And show me your feet," Petty said.

Destiny looked a little awkward, but she sat down on one of the sofas and pulled her sparkly black sandals off. Petty came closer and peered at her feet. "Aha!" she said. "Just as I thought. Rampant warts! Even after all these years . . . Yes . . . I definitely remember your fungal feet!"

"Eeeeeurgh!" went the audience.

And then Petty clapped her hand across her brow. "Of course!" she cried out, spinning around to face her old enemy. "I forgot Destiny because YOU burned out bits of my memory. It's YOUR fault, Victor Crouch! You are my ENEMY, and you're not going to get away with it!"

Victor attempted more shoulder patting and said: "It doesn't matter now, Petty, because

Destiny and I still *love* you . . ."

The audience went "Aaaaaaaaah!"

". . . And we're going to take you to a happy, safe place . . . where we can get to know each other again."

Three burly men, this time dressed in white coats, stepped onto the stage. Josh and Danny sat bolt upright in their seats. This was going wrong. *Badly* wrong.

"We're taking you to a lovely hospital to help you get better, Mommy," purred Destiny. "And you can still do all sorts of fun experiments while you're there. You can even have your little helpers come along with you. And guess what? They're here today!"

And then the cameras swung around to the audience, and Josh and Danny saw their own awestruck faces staring out of the screen at the back of the stage.

"Victor Crouch is after US too!" gasped Josh. "QUICK! Get DOWN!"

Josh and Danny threw themselves under the legs of the audience and slid through the gap in the seats, amid much shouting and squealing.

"Help us! Help us, audience!" called out Destiny. "Little Josh and Danny have to be caught and helped! They've been contaminated by my mother's experiments and need hospital treatment NOW!"

There was uproar. People started grabbing for the boys as they scrambled through the scaffolding until they reached the grass. In a gap between someone's legs, Danny watched as Petty was seized by the men in white coats.

"S.W.I.T.C.H.! We have to S.W.I.T.C.H.!" he yelled to Josh.

"What—HERE? In public?" Josh squawked.

"YES! We have to cause a HUGE distraction

or they're going to get Petty and lock her away and we'll never see her again!" Danny hauled the S.W.I.T.C.H. spray out of his jeans pocket. "And then they'll come for US!"

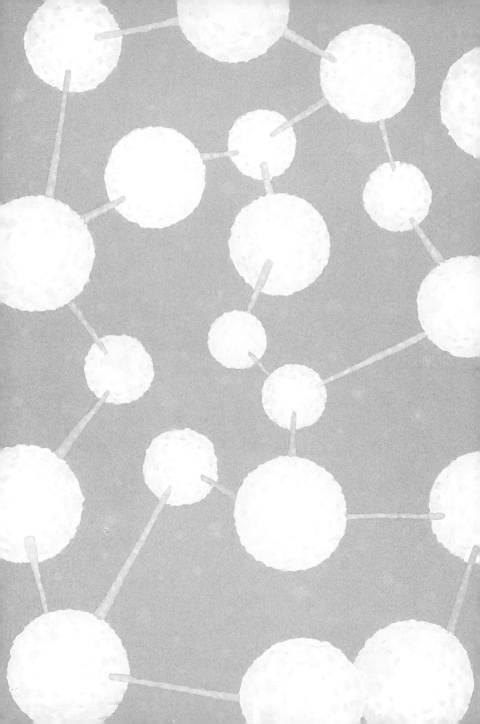

See Ya Later, Alligator

"GO!" Josh said. A second later, the S.W.I.T.C.H. spray hit him. Danny sprayed himself and pushed the bottle back into the case. Stashing it under his T-shirt, he saw that Josh was an alligator again. And FURIOUS. Josh's long, strong tail swished back and forth. He lost no time running out from under the seats as he thundered toward the stage, roaring with rage. Danny came hot on his brother's scaly heels.

The audience screamed with fear. Two *huge* alligators appeared out of nowhere and careened towards Destiny Darcy and her guests. Josh saw one of the men in white coats freeze, his mouth falling open in terror. Josh climbed onto the stage and ran for him, snapping at his heels. The man squealed and staggered offstage.

Destiny leaped onto one of the leather couches and shrieked for her burly security men. But they had all fled in horror. The audience, too, stormed out of the tent, falling over one another. Those still standing were shoving others out of the way to reach the exit first. Only a couple of cameramen stayed to film the action. Josh's and Danny's antics showed on the big screen behind them. Their tough brown scales gleamed in the bright lights.

Josh and Danny roared even more. They opened their huge jaws, showing off their many rows of teeth. They bellowed loudly. Victor Crouch sank into the sofa next to Petty, covering his face with sweaty fingers. One of his penciled-in eyebrows rubbed off.

"HELP! HELP! HELP MEEEEEE!" Destiny shrieked, as Josh brought his jaws crashing down on the leather sofa she was standing on. She fell into the corner and flapped her legs and arms, wailing, "I don't waaaant to get eaten by a crocodile! Noooooooooo!"

"It's NOT a crocodile, Dessy!" snapped Petty. "It's an alligator! Surely you know the difference, child?"

Destiny's foot smelled pretty good—warts or not! Josh reckoned it would be a lot like gnawing on a chicken drumstick. He grunted, grinned, and went to take a bite.

"JOSH! Is that YOU?"

Josh looked up at Petty and nodded, grinning madly with his snaggly teeth.

"Well, stop that AT ONCE!"

Petty stood over him. "I will NOT allow you to eat my daughter, no matter how much she deserves it." Josh closed his mouth and stepped back, feeling rather ashamed. It was the Piddle incident all over again.

"DANNY!" called Petty. "You CAN eat Victor if you want. That is perfectly acceptable."

Victor Crouch squeaked and then fainted, rolling sideways off the sofa.

"NOOO!" yelled Destiny. "MOM! Don't you remember? He's your friend!"

Petty sighed. "There are many things I don't remember, Destiny. Like you, for instance . . . although you're starting to look a bit more familiar. But one thing I will NEVER forget is that Victor Crouch is my DEADLY ENEMY. One day I will try to prove it to you . . . to the whole world. But for now . . . I must go."

Danny's teeth were about to sink into Victor's bony leg when Josh bellowed "DANNY! Stop it! You're not a real alligator—remember!"

"Come on, boys," said Petty. "I think it's time we got out of here." They made their way down from the stage and out across the tent, which was now empty. Even the cameramen had finally run away. There was still plenty of screaming and shouting going on outside. There were some emergency sirens in the distance too.

Petty paused at the tent exit and looked back at Victor Crouch, who was now groggily sitting up again. "A good try, Victor!" she called. "Convincing my daughter to help you trap me. And luring Danny and Josh here so that you could trap them too. But we're too smart for that! You may have gotten ahold of my marbles. But you

can't understand the S.W.I.T.C.H. formula code in them, can you? And you will NEVER get the solution from me. NEVER! NEVEEEEEEEEER!"

"PETTY! You NEED ME!" Victor bellowed back. "I can help you! I can bring you back to the secret government labs! Can't you see that you're just TOO DANGEROUS when you're left to work alone? For pity's sake, woman—you're working with eight-year-olds!"

Josh and Danny turned and grunted at Victor, who shrieked and fainted again.

"Wait!" Suddenly Destiny was running towards Petty. "Mommy—don't leave me! Not again!"

"Why would I stay, you soft-in-the-head TV twit?" thundered Petty. "You are a traitor to your own mother!"

"But . . . it's not the way it seems," sniffed Destiny. "You left your marbles with me . . . years ago," she said, her eyes darting nervously down at the two alligators at Petty's feet. "I don't know why . . . but you left me six of them."

Petty suddenly thumped her forehead. "Of course I did!" she said. "Of course! I left them

with you for safekeeping! I remember now! Rather stupid, though, wasn't it? You just handed them over to Victor Crouch!"

"Oh, Mother . . . it wasn't like that!" protested Destiny, her eyes filling with tears. "I was trying to think of ways to make you remember me. Every time I went to your house, you'd accuse me of trying to sell you replacement windows and slam the door in my face! So Victor asked if I had any keepsakes from you . . . something we could use. Then we realized what the marbles really were!"

"But he didn't know how to use them without me!" said Petty. "I bet he took them away for a while, didn't he? To 'examine' them. And then came back with this insane plan when he realized he couldn't make the S.W.I.T.C.H. code into formula on his own!"

Destiny gulped. "Yes . . . I suppose he did.
I'm sorry—but I thought he was right. That you
needed to be in a safe place . . . for people who are
a bit mad. I thought we might make you better."

"So, you were going to chuck me in a loony bin?"
snapped Petty. "And what about Josh and Danny?"

"Well, er, I didn't really think we'd lock up Josh
and Danny too," Destiny said, guiltily. "But I was
a bit worried at the way you kept turning them
into reptiles. It didn't seem terribly safe . . ."

"Well, *you* might not have locked them up,"
Petty said. "But Victor would. You don't know
him like I do!"

At this point, there were two thuds. Josh and
Danny S.W.I.T.C.H.ed back into boys. Danny was
still hissing with his jaws wide open. Destiny gave
them both a watery smile.

"Really," Destiny said, "we only got Josh and
Danny involved because you trust them." She
sniffed. "And you don't trust me."

"So it was *you* who followed us around,
dropping marble clues into our lives?" Josh said
accusingly to Destiny. "At our house, at our

school—at Princessland! You even followed us to Cornwall on our holiday!"

"Well . . . it wasn't always me," Destiny said. "I mean . . . I have lots of people I pay to do things for me. You don't think it was me who put marbles in that owl's nest? Or up in the light in your school gym, do you? Although it *was* me who sent you the marble in the parachute. I thought that was rather good . . ." She grinned smugly.

"Yes—it was!" admitted Danny, slipping Josh the case. "But today was just nuts. Who do you think you are, kidnapping Petty and putting her on your stupid TV show?"

"Your whole plan was ridiculous," added Petty. "You even acted it out in front of a studio audience!"

Destiny sighed. "I can't help it . . . it's such great TV!"

"You're dim, Destiny," sighed Petty. "Always were. Nice enough . . . but dim."

"At least I'm fabulously rich and famous," pointed out Destiny. "And maybe I wouldn't ever have become Destiny Darcy, TV star, if I'd been as clever as you are. But anyway . . . take this."

Destiny put the last MAMMALSWITCH marble—
an orange one—into Petty's hand and closed her
fingers over it. "The others onstage are just ordinary
marbles. For effect," she said. "This is the last one.
I don't think I should keep it. You *did* just stop me
from being eaten by a croc—I mean, an alligator . . ."

There was another anguished shout behind them.
"DESTINY!" wailed Victor, staggering across the
stage. "Don't let her GO!" He stumbled across the
stage—and then slipped on a marble and landed flat
on his face. His wig fell off, revealing his bald head.

"Go," said Destiny, her eyes shining. "And one
day, come back and tell me what happened next!
Maybe we can do a follow-up show . . ."

Petty raised one eyebrow, pocketing the final marble. "Erm . . . Josh, Danny . . . could you cause a distraction so I can slip away unnoticed?"

Josh and Danny grinned. Five seconds later, Petty smiled and gave their scaly snouts a pat. "You won't see me for a while . . . but I will be in touch . . ." she whispered.

Danny and Josh rushed out of the tent and caused an uproar. The two huge alligators thundered through the terrified crowd, made for the lake, and plunged into the water. Petty Potts slipped away unnoticed.

Watery Wonder

Josh and Danny had been underwater before . . .
as great diving beetles, frogs, and even anacondas.
But this . . . was something else!

Leaving the uproar behind them, they slid
swiftly down into the lake, sending a flock of
freaked-out ducks high into the air above them.
In just seconds, all that could be seen of the
alligators were two long wakes in the water,
fading fast as they paddled away.

The noise of the crowd was replaced by the
gurgling, booming, singing serenity of their
underwater world. Josh and Danny tucked their
legs in close to their bodies and undulated
through the water at speed. It felt cool and silky

and wonderful as they powered along with almost no effort. Bright autumn sunlight shafted down through the water, flickering fingers of gold through the greenish-blue haze.

Fish darted away from them. A few alarmed deep-diving birds sped back up to the surface in plumes of bubbles. But Josh and Danny weren't after snacks. They were just thrilled to be swimming alligators, kings of their domain, absolutely unstoppable!

They almost forgot the madness that had led them here. It was, without a doubt, their most exhilarating S.W.I.T.C.H. ever.

"You know . . . I could stay like this," Danny said. He turned over in the water, spinning his body around and around as he moved like a log in a river. His lower parts were paler—almost yellowy—compared with the chocolate-brown upper parts. And there was muscular ribbing all the way down his throat and chest.

"We could make a gator hole as a den," Josh said.

"Ooh—what's that? Sounds good," replied Danny, still gently rotating in the water. He knew this was something alligators did when they had prey in their jaws, to drown it before eating it.

"Alligators dig right into banks, sometimes, and make these sort-of caves," explained Josh. "Right up under the bank where nobody can find them."

"That would be amazing!" Danny said. "We should make one now!"

"Yeah . . ." said Josh, his tail arching lazily in the water behind him. "But we haven't really got enough time. Any second we're going to—"

SPLOOSH!

"—S.W.I.T.C.H. back," gasped Josh as soon as his head was above water.

Danny climbed onto the bank, taking the case from his brother so Josh could get himself out as well. "We could always have another go . . ."

"Not now," Josh said, looking at his watch (happily a waterproof one). "We'd better get back."

They climbed out in the farthest corner of the lake and made their way back home, keeping well away from the crowds and the yellow tents and the police on the other side of the lake. They spotted an animal-control van too. Obviously, the hunt for the alligators was on.

Back at home, they got into the house and managed to shower, dry off, and change before Jenny had even finished watching TV. The *Darcy Show* episode she was watching had been recorded some time ago. So she had no idea about the amazing show she had just missed in her own town.

"So," Danny said as he made cups of tea in the kitchen. "Do you think we'll ever see Petty again?"

"Not for a while," Josh said, cutting them both a bit of ginger cake. "But one day—definitely. After all"—he pointed to the lunchbox on the table—"we've still got the whole S.W.I.T.C.H. spray set."

"We'd better hide it—really well," Danny said. "In case Victor Crouch comes after us again."

"Yes," agreed Josh. "But on the other hand . . . if he does come after us, we probably should have just a little bit of S.W.I.T.C.H. spray on us. "We'll never know when we might need it . . ."

Top Secret!

For Petty Potts's Eyes Only!!

DIARY ENTRY 701

SUBJECT: My Destiny

Well, back to pen and paper. It will be a long time before I dare to return to my lab and use my computer again. What a good thing I had the brilliance of mind to hide all the BUGSWITCH and REPTOSWITCH cubes, along with the new MAMMALSWITCH marbles, in a very, very secret place, nowhere near my old lab or my new one!

I guess I'll be on the run for a while now. I can't be sure whether Victor Crouch really can get the government to hunt me down. But I wouldn't put it past the eyebrowless freak! If he tells them everything he knows, they'll certainly want the S.W.I.T.C.H. project for themselves. And I'm not ready to hand it over!

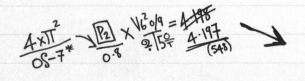

But I WILL return. I WILL get back to Josh and Danny and work on the MAMMALSWITCH formula. And who knows, maybe I will one day return to Destiny and tell her everything. Imagine—I've had a daughter all these years! A TV star too . . .

In the meantime, I hope Victor doesn't go after Josh and Danny . . . but I think they can look after themselves for now while I work out a plan to put him out of action . . . for GOOD. Oh yes . . . for GOOD!

Bwah-ha-ha-ha-ha-haaaa!!! Bwah-ha-ha-ha-ha-haaaa!!!

Is that spelled right? A deranged cackle is SO hard to get down on paper . . .

$$\frac{60}{\frac{OUP}{\pi}} \to \cancel{\beta} \to \frac{1}{2}St$$

Recommended Reading

BOOKS

Want to brush up on your reptile and amphibian knowledge? Here's a list of books dedicated to slithering and hopping creatures.

Johnson, Jinny. *Animal Planet™ Wild World: An Encyclopedia of Animals.* Minneapolis: Millbrook Press, 2013.

McCarthy, Colin. *Reptile.* DK Eyewitness Books. New York: DK Publishing, 2012.

Parker, Steve. *Pond & River.* DK Eyewitness Books. New York: DK Publishing, 2011.

WEBSITES

Find out more about nature and wildlife using the websites below.

National Geographic Kids

http://kids.nationalgeographic.com/kids

Go to this website to watch videos and read facts about your favorite reptiles and amphibians.

San Diego Zoo Kids

http://kids.sandiegozoo.org/animals
Curious to learn more about some of the coolest-looking reptiles and amphibians? This website has lots of information and stunning pictures of some of Earth's most interesting creatures.

US Fish & Wildlife Service

http://www.nwf.org/wildlife/wildlife-library
/amphibians-reptiles-and-fish.aspx
Want some tips to help you look for wildlife in your own neighborhood? Learn how to identify some slimy creatures and some scaly ones as well.

CHECK OUT ALL OF THE

S.W.I.T.C.H.

Spider Stampede
by Ali Sparkes Illustrated by Ross Collins

S.W.I.T.C.H.

Ant Attack
by Ali Sparkes Illustrated by Ross Collins

S.W.I.T.C.H.

Fly Frenzy
by Ali Sparkes Illustrated by Ross Collins

S.W.I.T.C.H.

Crane Fly Crash
by Ali Sparkes Illustrated by Ross Collins

S.W.I.T.C.H.

Grasshopper Glitch
by Ali Sparkes Illustrated by Ross Collins

S.W.I.T.C.H.

Beetle Blast
by Ali Sparkes Illustrated by Ross Collins

 **TITLES!**

Frog Freakout
by Ali Sparkes Illustrated by Ross Collins

Newt Nemesis #8
by Ali Sparkes Illustrated by Ross Collins

Lizard Loopy #9
by Ali Sparkes
Illustrated by Ross Collins

Chameleon Chaos #10
by Ali Sparkes
Illustrated by Ross Collins

Turtle Terror #11
by Ali Sparkes Illustrated by Ross Collins

Gecko Gladiator #12
by Ali Sparkes Illustrated by Ross Collins

Anaconda Adventure #13
by Ali Sparkes Illustrated by Ross Collins

Alligator Action #14
by Ali Sparkes Illustrated by Ross Collins

About the Author

Ali Sparkes grew up in the wilds of the New Forest, raised by sand lizards who taught her the secret language of reptiles and how to lick her own eyes.

At least, that's how Ali remembers it. Her family argues that she grew up in a house in Southampton, raised by her mom and dad, who taught her the not terribly secret language of English and wished she'd stop chewing her hair.

She once caught a slow worm. It flicked around like mad, and she was a bit scared and dropped it.

Ali still lives in Southampton, now with her husband and two sons. She likes to hang out in the nearby wildlife center spying on common lizards. The lizards are considering legal action . . .

About the Illustrator

Ross Collins's more than eighty picture books and books for young readers have appeared in print around the world. He lives in Scotland and, in his spare time, enjoys leaning backward precariously in his chair.